JUNE SOBEL

B Is for Bulldozer
A CONSTRUCTION ABC

ILLUSTRATED BY
MELISSA IWAI

GULLIVER BOOKS
HARCOURT, INC.
San Diego   New York   London

Library of Congress Cataloging-in-Publication Data
Sobel, June.
B is for bulldozer: a construction ABC/by June Sobel;
illustrated by Melissa Iwai.
p.   cm.
"Gulliver Books."
Summary: As children watch over the course of a year,
builders construct a roller coaster using tools and materials
that begin with each letter of the alphabet.
[1. Roller coasters—Fiction.   2. Building—Fiction.   3. Construction
equipment—Fiction.   4. Alphabet.   5. Stories in rhyme.]
I. Iwai, Melissa, ill.   II. Title.
PZ7.S685228Bi   2003
[E]—dc21   2001006869
ISBN 0-15-202250-3

H G F E D C

Manufactured in China

The illustrations in this book were done in acrylic on board.
The text type was set in Bernhard Gothic Medium.
The display type was set in Bernhard Antique and Stencil.
Color separations by Colourscan Co. Pte. Ltd., Singapore
Manufactured by South China Printing Company, Ltd., China
This book was printed on totally chlorine-free Enso Stora Matte paper.
Production supervision by Sandra Grebenar and Ginger Boyer
Designed by Linda Lockowitz

To Adam Raudonis—
my inspiration

—J. S.

For my dad,
the best builder I know

—M. I.

Do you see the Asphalt
for paving the road,

Nearby there's a Forklift
hauling a pole.

Let's look for
the Grader
on the roadbed,

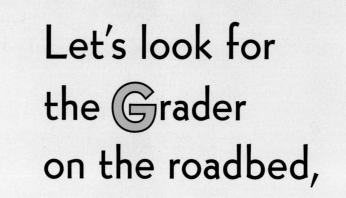

and a man with a
Hard hat protecting
his head.

I spy an ▌ beam made out of steel,

guiding the **P**ipes
into the holes.

The welders won't Quit
till the metal is bent,

Our eXcitement grows—
we're ready for fun!

For more than a Year we've watched the park bloom.